I0889243

Team Stats—Basketball Edition

BOSTON CELTICS

Nicki Clausen-Grace
and Jeff Grace

BLACK RABBIT BOOKS

Bolt is published by Black Rabbit Books
P.O. Box 3263, Mankato, Minnesota, 56002.
www.blackrabbitbooks.com
Copyright © 2021 Black Rabbit Books

Jennifer Besel, editor; Michael Sellner, designer;
Omay Ayres, photo researcher

All rights reserved. No part of this book may be reproduced, stored in a retrieval system or transmitted in any form or by any means, electronic, mechanical, photocopying, recording, or otherwise, without written permission from the publisher.

Library of Congress Cataloging-in-Publication Data
Names: Clausen-Grace, Nicki, author. | Grace, Jeff, 1967- author.
Title: Boston Celtics / Nicki Clausen-Grace and Jeff Grace.
Description: Mankato, Minnesota : Black Rabbit Books, 2021. | Series: Bolt. Team stats, basketball edition | Includes bibliographical references and index. | Audience: Ages 8-12 | Audience: Grades 4-6 |
Summary: "Discover the Boston Celtics' powerhouse players and biggest moments through exciting text and dynamic infographics"— Provided by publisher.
Identifiers: LCCN 2019045881 (print) | LCCN 2019045882 (ebook) | ISBN 9781623102883 (hardcover) | ISBN 9781644663844 (paperback) | ISBN 9781623103828 (ebook)
Subjects: LCSH: Boston Celtics (Basketball team)—Juvenile literature. | Basketball players—Massachusetts—Boston—Biography—Juvenile literature.
Classification: LCC GV885.52.B67 C53 2021 (print) | LCC GV885.52.B67 (ebook) | DDC 796.323/640974461—dc23
LC record available at https://lccn.loc.gov/2019045881
LC ebook record available at https://lccn.loc.gov/2019045882

Printed in the United States. 2/20

All facts and statistics are current as of the 2018–2019 season.

Image Credits

Alamy: Archive PL, 24; AP Images: ASSOCIATED PRESS, 18, 28–29; Dave Tenenbaum, 4–5; ED WIDDIS, 22; Frank C. Curtin, 19; H. RUMPH JR, 23; Mary Schwalm, 8–9; Michael Dwyer, Cover; Winslow Townson, 10, 17; Dreamstime: Ferit Aksit, 6–7; Jerry Coli, 3, 18; Maxim Grebeshkov, 9; ebay.com: plaquelady, 7; Getty: AAron Ontiveroz, 26–27; Bettmann, 7, 13, 14–15, 21, 25; Boston Globe, 22, 23; MediaNews Group/Boston Herald via Getty Images, 26; Newscom: MIKE SEGAR/REUTERS, 10–11; Shutterstock: Duda Vasilii, 28–29; EFKS, Cover, 1, 22–23; GOLFX, 31; IfH, Cover; vasosh, 9, 16, 28–29, 32
Every effort has been made to contact copyright holders for material reproduced in this book. Any omissions will be rectified in subsequent printings if notice is given to the publisher.

CONTENTS

PISTONS
45
33

CHAPTER 1

On the COURT

The score was 107–106, with the Detroit Pistons in the lead. Boston Celtics player Larry Bird stole a pass. He tossed it to Dennis Johnson. Johnson put in a **layup** with one second left on the clock. The Celtics took Game 5 of the 1987 Eastern Conference Finals. The "Luck of the Irish" had struck again.

CHAPTER 2

History of the CELTICS

The Celtics team is from Boston, Massachusetts. It formed in 1946. The owner thought about naming the team the Whirlwinds, Olympics, or Unicorns. But he decided on the Celtics. The Celts were an **ancient** group of people in Ireland. A lot of Irish people lived in Boston. So the name made sense.

The Celtics' mascot is Lucky the Leprechaun.

1946 team

CELTICS By the Numbers

56 number of playoff appearances

173 most points team scored in one game

24
team record for
number of 3-pointers
made in one game
23
number of
retired
jerseys

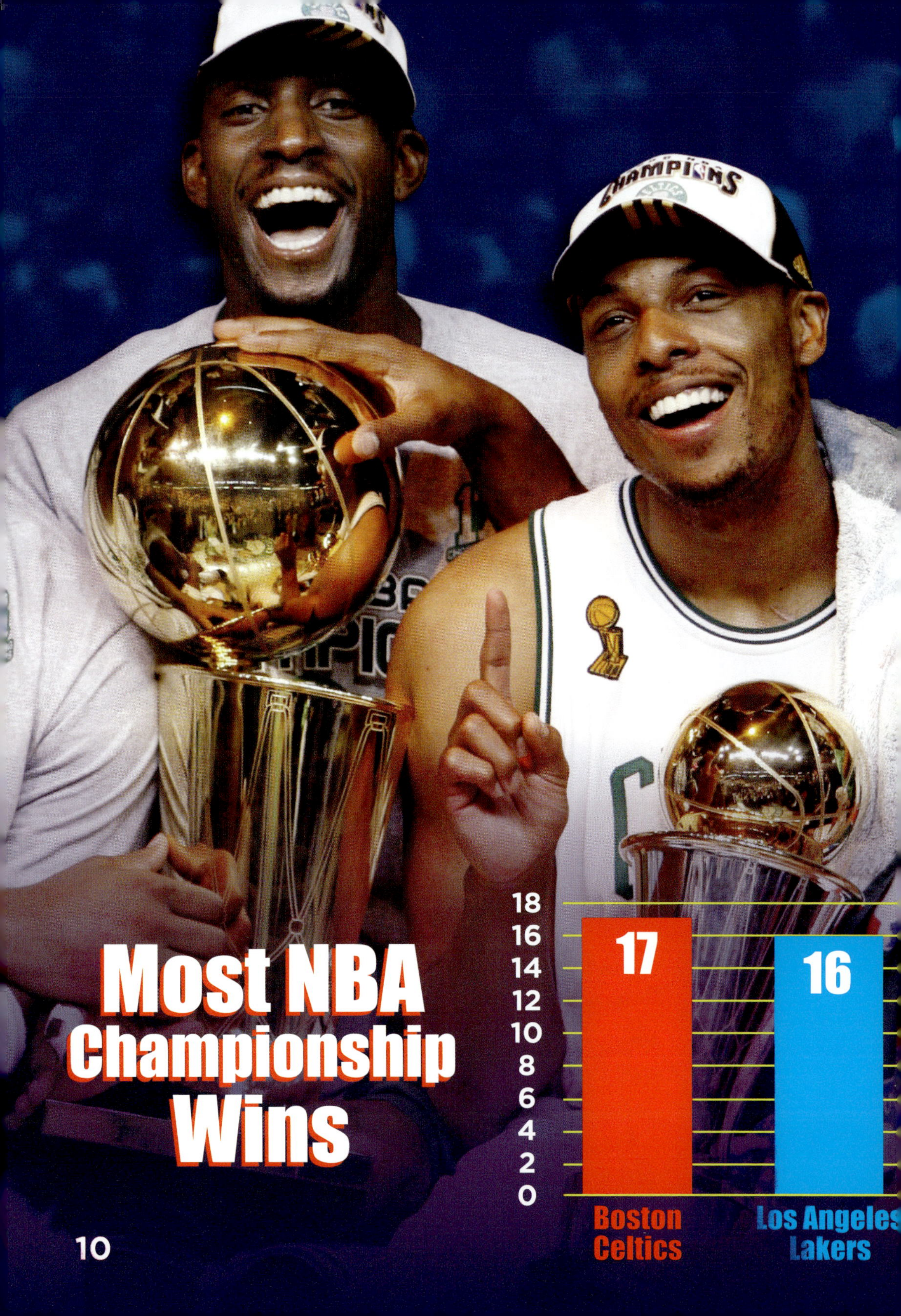

Most NBA Championship Wins

Success and Money

The team has been very successful. In fact, it has won more championships than any other NBA team.

Its success has made the team popular. In 2018, the Celtics were worth $2.8 billion. It had the fifth-highest **net worth** in the NBA. Teams make money through ticket sales and TV deals. They also sell items with the team **logo** on them.

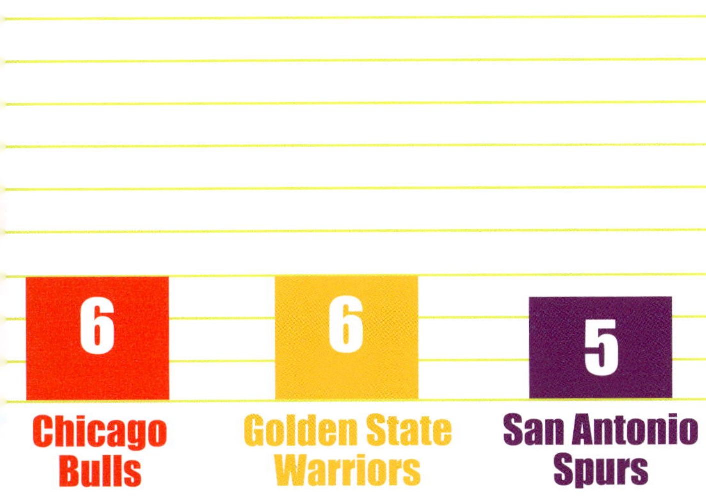

CHAPTER 3

Greatest MOMENTS

The Celtics has had many incredible moments. One of those times was in the 1957 Finals. The series was tied. The Celtics and St. Louis Hawks both wanted to win the seventh game. The winner would get the championship.

The game was a battle. In double overtime, the Celtics led 125–123. A Hawks player took a shot with one second left. It rolled off the rim. Celtics players and fans went crazy. They won their first championship.

No other Game 7 has ever gone into two overtimes.

Picking a Winner

Great teams are made up of great players. NBA coaches and fans are happy when they can sign the best ballers. The Celtics chose Larry Bird in the first round of the 1978 draft. He was a perfect choice for the team. He won the **Rookie** of the Year award his first season. And he went on to lead the team to three championships. Fans look back on his draft as a fantastic moment.

Champions Again

In 2008, the Celtics played the Los Angeles Lakers in the title series. The Celtics had won three games. The Lakers had two wins. If the Celtics won the sixth game, it would win its 17th championship. Boston took control of the game. At halftime, it was up 58–35. For the rest of the game, the Lakers trailed by 24 points or more.

CHAMPIONS
2008 NBA CHAMPIONS
CELTICS

Havlicek's Team Records

26,395
most career points

1,270
most career games played

46,471
most career minutes played

CHAPTER 4

CELTICS Superstars

The Celtics' biggest moments wouldn't have happened without great players. John Havlicek was one of the best. He played both guard and forward in his 16 seasons with the team. With Havlicek, the team won eight NBA championships. He played in 13 NBA All-Star Games.

Larry Bird

At 6 feet, 9 inches (2 meters) tall, Larry Bird always stood out. But it wasn't his height that made people notice him. Bird was an amazing player. He holds the Celtics record for most career triple-doubles. And he won MVP awards three seasons in a row.

triple-double — scoring at least 10 points, 10 rebounds, and 10 **assists** in a game

CELTICS
33
Radio
Tape
50
CELTIC

CELTICS COACHES

No matter how good the players are, they need good coaches. The Celtics has had some of the best.

	Red Auerbach
years coaching Celtics	16
regular-season wins with Celtics	795
NBA championship wins with Celtics	9

TOM HEINSOHN

RED AUERBACH

Tom Heinsohn	K. C. Jones	Doc Rivers
9	5	9
427	308	416
2	2	1

K. C. JONES

DOC RIVERS

Bill Russell

As soon as someone shoots, players scramble to get the ball. If the shot misses, getting the ball is called a rebound. Bill Russell was a fantastic rebounder. He played about 50 years ago. But he still holds team rebound records. He grabbed 21,620 career rebounds.

Bob Cousy

Basketball is a team sport. Players need to help each other score. Bob Cousy was good at that. He had 28 assists in just one 1959 game. His 6,945 career assists is a team record.

Jaylen Brown

Continuing the Tradition

Today's Celtics players continue to push for wins. Players like Gordon Hayward and Jaylen Brown impress fans. The Celtics has a strong history. Fans look forward to more great moments to come.

CELTICS TIMELINE

1946 — The team forms.

1957 — Team wins its first NBA championship.

1960 — Russell grabs 51 rebounds in a game.

Team drafts Bird.
1978
1985
Bird scores 60 points in a game.
2008
Celtics win its 17th NBA championship.

GLOSSARY

ancient (AYN-shunt)—from a time long ago

assist (uh-SIST)—the action, such as a pass, of a player who helps a teammate to score

layup (LAY-uhp)—a shot in basketball made from near the basket usually by playing the ball off the backboard

logo (LO-go)—a symbol used to identify a company

mascot (MAH-scaht)—a person, animal, or object adopted by a group as a symbolic figure especially to bring them good luck

net worth (NEHT WURTH)—the amount of money someone would have after selling everything and paying all their bills

retired (ree-TAHY-urhd)—withdrawn from active use

riot (RAHY-uht)—a gathering where people behave in a violent and uncontrolled way

rookie (ROOK-ee)—a first-year player

BOOKS

Gigliotti, Jim. *Boston Celtics.* Insider's Guide to Pro Basketball. Mankato, MN: Child's World, 2019.

Weakland, Mark. *Basketball Records.* All-Time Sports Records. Mankato, MN: Black Rabbit Books, 2021.

Whiting, Jim. *Boston Celtics.* The NBA: A History of Hoops. Mankato, MN: Creative Education, 2018.

WEBSITES

Basketball
www.ducksters.com/sports/basketball.php

Boston Celtics
www.nba.com/celtics/

Boston Celtics Facts for Kids
kids.kiddle.co/Boston_Celtics

INDEX